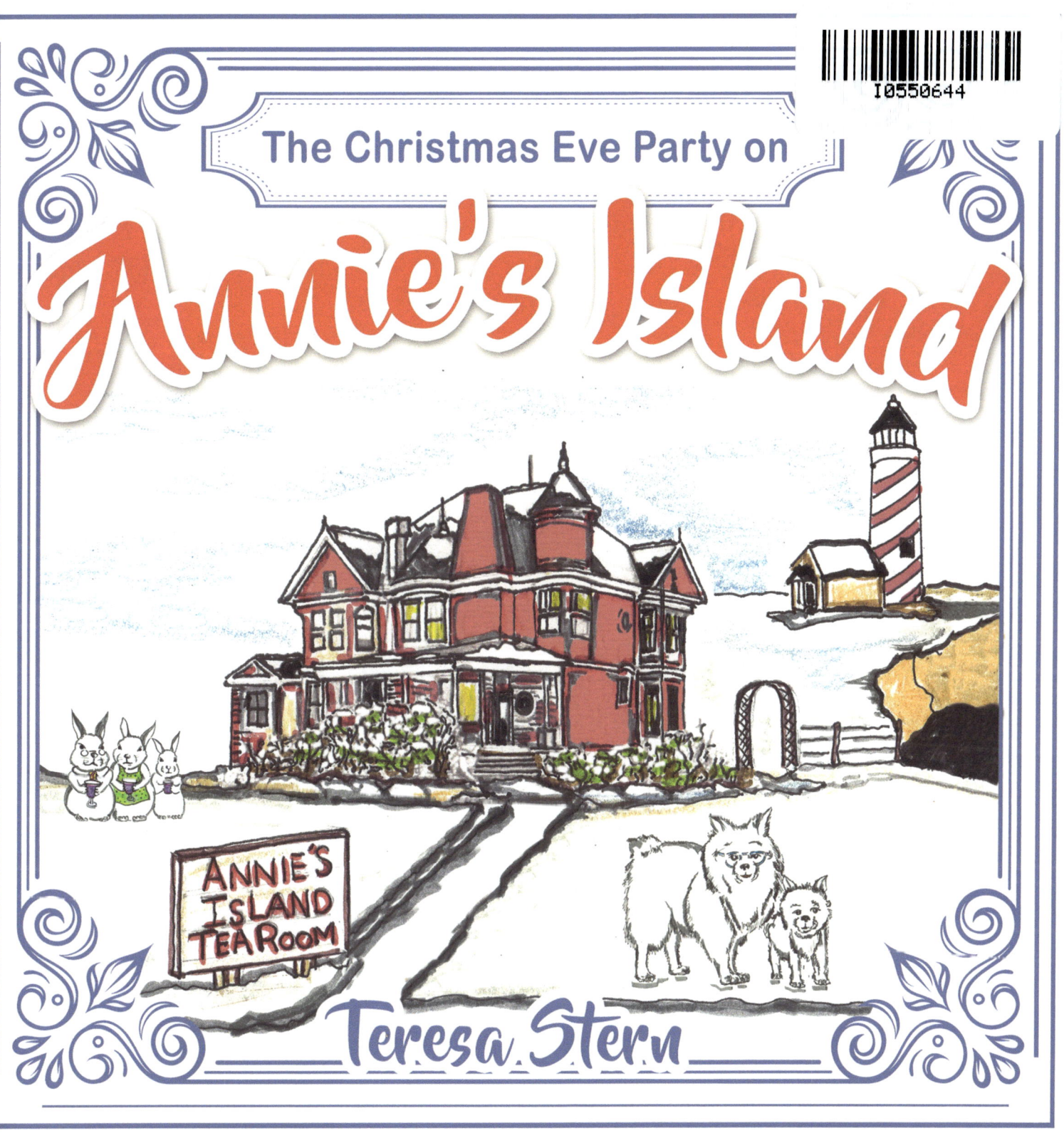

The Christmas Eve Party on

Annie's Island

ANNIE'S ISLAND TEA ROOM

Teresa Stern

I0550644

Copyright 2018 by Teresa Stern
Published by Teresa Ann Stern
2310 Deer Run Cir, Brownsville, TX 78521
teresastern_1836@yahoo.com
ISBN: 978-1-7334187-0-6

All rights reserved. No part of this publication may be reproduced,

stored in a retrieval system or transmitted, in any form, or by any means,

electronic, mechanical, recorded, photocopied, or otherwise without the prior

written permission of both the copyright owner and the above-mentioned publisher

of this book, except by a reviewer who may quote brief passages in a review.

The scanning, uploading, and distribution of this book via the Internet or via any other

means without the permission of the publisher is illegal and punishable by law. Please

purchase only authorized electronic editions and do not participate in or encourage

electronic piracy of copyrighted materials.

First Edition: January 2020

Illustrated by: Henry Chavez

Graphic Design Layout by: TAM Corbette L. & Juan Pablo Gomez

Edited by: Yolanda R. Carroll & Lupita Gomez

Printed in the United States of America

DEDICATIONS

I want to thank the following people that helped me with my book,

"The Christmas Eve Party on Annie's Island"

Maurice Jones for sharing the recipe for the scones, which belonged

to his mother, Doris Jones.

It would have been impossible to write this book without it.

Lebby Salinas, The Fooducator™, for teaching me how to substitute ingredients for vegan and gluten free options.

Fooducation Potluck and a Movie at Cine El Rey, Home Bakers Markets, and Growing Growers Farmers Market for allowing me to demonstrate my recipes and giving me the opportunity to sell my Vegan Gluten-Free Scones.

Teri Closner for helping me bake all the recipes that went into the book.

JC Saenz for encouraging me to rise to the challenge in converting an already perfect recipe to one that gives vegan or gluten-free options and for his willingness to play the part of official taste tester.

Thank you for putting the icing on the book Juan Pablo & Lupita Gómez

Thank you Juan & Aileen for being the best critics!

Pamela Foster (Downton Abbey Cooks) for the countless emails while doing my researching on the proper "afternoon tea". The information she shared with me was invaluable in putting this project together.

Lidia Fonseca; and in loving memory of her Pomeranian dog Yogi Bear.

Lastly, to those friends who have allowed me to include them in my story:

Barbara Storz, "The Garden Gal"; Pat Ozuna of Circle 3 Farm and Ranch; Isaac R Guerra of The Centennial Club; *Bert Guerra* of The Historic Cine El Rey Theater & Foundation; Dellanira Regalado, Andrea Jasmine Gonzalez and Shawn Elliot Russell.

I want to thank my family, all of my friends including my Facebook Friends for all your love and support while working on this book.

Love, Teresa

Henry and his parents live in a Victorian House off the coastline of Annie's Island. Henry's parents run a tea room from their home. The tea room is named after the island. The tea room has an English/Welsh feel to it. On the wall mantel, there is a model of a Xebec Mediterranean sailing ship that once belonged to Pat's father Admiral Billy Rabbit.

Walking through the entrance to the tea room there is a small bakery and shop area. The bakery is full of desserts and the traditional English/Welsh sweets such as The Welsh Cakes, Welsh Scones, Victorian Sponge Cake and Queen of Puddings.

In the shop area, there are a wide variety of tea kettles, teapots, tea sets, and tea products to make the perfect afternoon tea time.

Every Christmas Eve, Henry's parents close the tea room to have their traditional Christmas Eve afternoon tea with their family and then the Christmas Eve dinner with their close friends and neighbors that live on Annie's Island.

On December 23, after the tea room closed, Henry and his parents went to Storz's Market to buy groceries for the Christmas Eve dinner.

"Mommy, I want to make Godfather Captain Isaac Lion's Creamy Zucchini Soup," said Henry.

Mom said to Henry, "Your Grandfather, Admiral Billy Rabbit, and your dad served with Captain Isaac Lion in the Royal Navy. On a Christmas Holiday, our family went to your Godfather's house on King Bert's Island. Your Godfather made the best Creamy Zucchini Soup and told us it was his family recipe. That night your father and I asked Captain Isaac to be your Godfather, and as a 'thank you' present he gave us his family recipe for Creamy Zucchini Soup. I am going to teach you how to make it for the Christmas Eve dinner."

"That's a great story Mommy. Mommy, I will get a loaf of bread and some butter to go with Godfather Captain Isaac Lion's Creamy Zucchini Soup," said Henry.

While at the market, Henry and his parents got what they needed to make Captain Isaac Lion's Creamy Zucchini Soup,

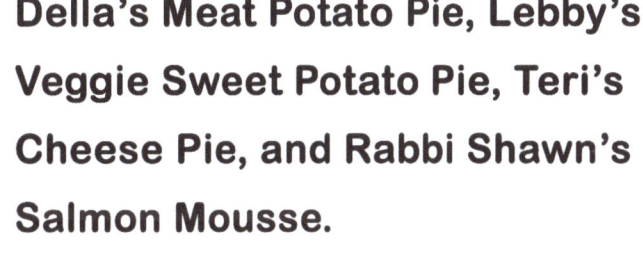

Della's Meat Potato Pie, Lebby's Veggie Sweet Potato Pie, Teri's Cheese Pie, and Rabbi Shawn's Salmon Mousse.

Before heading back to the tea room Henry and his parents stopped at Mrs. Badger's Vintage Shop to get some last-minute gifts. It is a tradition in Henry's Family to pass out Christmas Eve gifts to their friends and neighbors on Annie's Island.

3

Pat came across the cutest and the most beautiful quilts her eyes could imagine. Mrs. Badger said to Pat, "Each quilt has a story behind it." Pat asked Mrs. Badger, "What is the story behind your quilts?"

Mrs. Badger answered,"I made these quilts myself and it took many years to make them. My Mama kept pieces of clothing from all of her children. Those pieces of clothing were sewn into her quilts. Those quilts are called 'Memory Quilts'."

Pat said, "My grandmother has several quilts of her own and my mother made a quilt from my baby clothes."

Mrs. Badger continued to explain,"Quilts are special because the result is a patchwork of many different colors and fabrics. Each one is uniquely beautiful. Often, these quilts are passed from one generation to the next, and each generation adds to it. These quilts have been collected

4

over the years from my family,
my husband's family and our friends.
I bring them to my shop to sell
and pass on the memories."

Pat smiled and said, "Your quilts are very lovely.
I will take this red and black plaid bed quilt
for my new neighbor, Wiley Mink."

Henry and his dad were in the toy room.
Henry looked at Mrs. Badger and said,
"You have so many toys!
It reminds me of my Grandma's playroom."

"Henry Bunny Rabbit, what did you say?!" asked his Mom.

Mrs. Badger gave a little laugh, "No Worries!
Children say the most darling little things."

Henry spotted a box of yo-yos in the corner of the
toy room, "Dad look at all these yo-yos!"
Dad came over to look at the yo-yos.

"Dad, will you buy me a yo-yo please?"
asked Henry.

Dad smiled and said,
"It's up to your Mum!"

"Mommy, can I have a yo-yo?"
asked Henry.

"Yes Henry, you can have a yo-yo."
answered his Mother. Henry jumped for joy
and gave her a big hug.

"While we are here in the toy room,
you can pick out some toys
for your friends' Christmas Eve gifts."

While Henry's mother was paying for the
Christmas Eve gifts, Henry's father noticed
that Henry was holding a wooden soldier.

Henry asked his Dad,
"Will you buy me a toy soldier?"

Mrs. Badger said,
"That is not a toy soldier. You're holding a nutcracker. It is used to crack open a variety of nuts, such as walnuts and chestnuts. During the Christmas Holidays, there is a local Beaver on Annie's Island that makes the most beautiful nutcrackers you have ever seen. He brings them into my shop to sell. He said he is not doing it for the money but, to bring joy to others' lives. He comes from a family line of Nutcracker Makers. Over the years, I bought his nutcrackers to give as gifts to friends and family. My first Christmas on Annie's Island he gave me a nutcracker. Henry, you're holding the first Nutcracker he gave me when I first arrived on Annie's Island."

"Henry, can you please give Mrs. Badger back her nutcracker," said Dad. Henry handed the nutcracker back to Mrs. Badger and she put the nutcracker on the mantel next to the Christmas tree.When they arrived back at Annie's Tea Room, Henry and his parents went into the kitchen to prepare for the Christmas Eve dinner.

Henry was helping his Mother with his Godfather
Captain Isaac Lion's Creamy Zucchini Soup,
Della's Meat Potato Pie, Lebby's Veggie Sweet
Potato Pie and Teri's Cheese Pie.

Henry's Mother chopped and shredded the vegetables
and cheeses. Henry put the vegetables and cheeses
into bowls and Mom helped Henry with the lids.
Mom told Henry to get a marker and masking tape to
label each bowl of the vegetables and cheeses
to match the dish they're making for the Christmas
Eve dinner.

Mom also said each dish should have a certain
number of ingredients, vegetables, and cheeses and
that this is part of cooking and doing this makes
cooking much easier. Henry then put the bowls into
the refrigerator. Dad prepared Rabbi Shawn's
Salmon Mousse while Henry received a math
lesson in cooking measurements.

Dad filled the salmon molds with salmon mousse and Henry helped Dad wrap the molds and place them into the refrigerator. Mom and Dad told Henry it's time for bed. They both tell him that Christmas Eve is a big day and there will be lots to do. Henry's parents tucked Henry into bed while Henry gave them both big hugs and kisses and he told his parents he loves both of them and he's going to dream about the Christmas Eve dinner.

Henry's parents smiled at him while turning off the light. On December 24, Christmas Eve morning after breakfast, Henry went to the linen cabinet to get the doilies, napkins, runner, and tablecloths for the Christmas Eve dinner.

Henry and his Mother went to the tea room to set up the tables. The tables and carts were decorated in Christmas and Hanukkah colors.

In the foyer, there was a Christmas tree and a Hanukkah Bush. Henry and his parents got the ornaments, lights, and decorations from the attic. They started decorating the Christmas tree and Hanukkah Bush. Over the years, the rabbit family had gone to the Ornaments Craft Day on Beatrix's Island where they made the most beautiful ornaments.

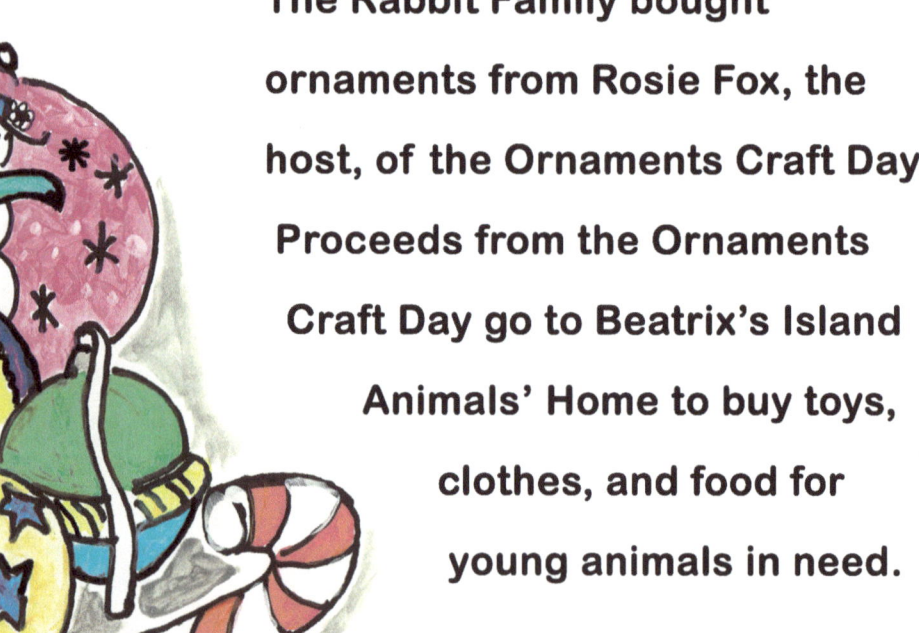

The Rabbit Family bought ornaments from Rosie Fox, the host, of the Ornaments Craft Day. Proceeds from the Ornaments Craft Day go to Beatrix's Island Animals' Home to buy toys, clothes, and food for young animals in need.

Mom tells Henry it's time to get started on the
Christmas Eve afternoon tea. Henry and his mother
are in the kitchen making Welsh Cakes and Welsh Scones.
Henry and his mother sing a Welsh song that has been sung for
many years while people made Welsh Cakes and Welsh Scones.

"Little Cakes, Little Scones"

"How round you are?"

"Little Cakes, Little Scones"

"How golden brown you are?"

"Little Cakes, Little Scones"

"How sweet you are?"

"Little Cakes, Little Scones"

"Tea time is waiting for you."

It was 4:00 p.m. when Henry's Grandmother arrived for
afternoon tea. In the drawing-room, there was a table set
by the fireplace. The table was set with a beautiful Christmas
tablecloth and matching napkins. There was a Christmas tea set
on the table. Henry's mother served her guests Christmas Tea
Blend tea, Welsh Cakes and Welsh Scones. Henry told his
Grandmother that he helped his mommy make the Welsh Cakes
and Welsh Scones. Henry and his mommy sang the Welsh Song
about the Welsh Sweets.

11

Pat's Mother told Henry,
"Your great-grandmother taught me the song and
I taught your Mommy, too. The Welsh Song is sung
only when making the Welsh Cakes and Welsh Scones
and it's a tradition on our Welsh side of the family."

"Wow! That is a great story Grandma," said Henry.

"I am glad you like it Henry," said Grandma.

It was 5:30 p.m. The Rabbit Family needed to prepare
the feast for the Christmas Eve dinner at 8:00 p.m.
Henry hugged and kissed his grandmother goodbye.
His grandmother told Henry she would see him
tomorrow for Christmas lunch.

After Henry's Grandmother left, Henry and
his parents went into the kitchen to prepare
the Christmas Eve dinner. Henry's father made
a dessert tier for the guests.

12

The doorbell rang at 7:30 p.m. and the guests began to arrive. The first guest to arrive was Wiley Mink, followed by Lidia Pomeranian and her son Yogi, and then Cal and Cate Cat with their twin kittens Casey and Callie.

"Welcome to our annual Christmas Eve dinner," said George Rabbit. "Come on in and follow me to the tea room."

Pat, George Rabbit and their son Henry greeted their guests. George gave a short speech, "Friends and neighbors, welcome to our annual Christmas Eve dinner. Tonight is special because it's not just Christmas Eve, it is also the first night of Hanukkah Enjoy the dinner."

The first course to come out was the Creamy Zucchini Soup.
Pat and George served the soup while Henry said,
"It's named after my Godfather Captain Isaac Lion who made
the best Creamy Zucchini soup ever in the Royal Navy and
my Mommy taught me how to make it."

The guests gave out a hearty laugh and said, "Bravo!"
Wiley Mink told Henry the soup is delicious and his Godfather
would be so proud of him for making his famous
Creamy Zucchini Soup.

Henry replied,
"Thank you, Mr. Mink."

Pat said, "The second courses are

Della's Meat Potato Pie

and Lebby's Veggie Sweet Potato Pie.

These dishes are named after

two of my friends, Della Bluebird and Lebby Butterfly.

My two friends couldn't be here tonight

because they are at a charity dinner with Rosie Fox.

They are raising money for the young animals

that live at the Beatrix Island Animals' Home.

My friend Rosie Fox hosts an Ornaments Craft Day on

Beatrix Island and proceeds go to the Beatrix Island

Animals' Home. My family have been to Rosie Fox's

Ornaments Craft Day and even bought ornaments from her.

Let me play the video messages from Della Blue Bird

and Lebby Butterfly.

"**Hello**,
my name is Lebby Butterfly…"

"… and my name is Della Bluebird."

(In chorus)
"We are friends of Pat Rabbit."

"Della and I couldn't be there tonight on Annie's Island for The Rabbit's Annual Christmas Eve dinner. We are looking forward to next year's Christmas Eve dinner. Lebby, JC, and, I and my daughter Jasmine Worm want to wish you all a Merry Christmas and Happy New Year!" said Della. "Mommy!" "Yes, Jasmine." "JC and I want to sing 'I Wish You a Merry Christmas!' "Jasmine and JC, then sang, "I Wish You a Merry Christmas."
"I have something to tell everyone," said JC Caterpillar.
"My Christmas Wish came true… Lebby Butterfly is going to be my new Mommy! Now, let's eat scones."
"That's my sweet boy!" said Lebby.

After the video ended, Pat, George, Henry and the guests clapped.

16

"Being the first night of Hanukkah my husband George made two special Hanukkah dishes for the Cat Family. They are named after Rabbi Shawn and his wife Teri Butterfly now living in Israel. Rabbi Shawn's Salmon Mousse and Teri's Cheese Potato Pie. Teri is Lebby Butterfly's cousin. Bon Appétit!" said Pat Rabbit.

The other guests turned to The Cats Family and wished them all a Happy Hanukkah.

Cal and Cate said to George, "The Salmon Mousse and the Cheese Potato Pie are just wonderful and our twins love it."

"I am glad you like them," replied George.

17

The guests were finishing their dinner when

George came out and asked, "Who is ready for sweets?"

The children yelled in unison,

"Yay! **They then ran up to**

We want Sweets!" **the sweets cart.**

On the cart, there was a three-tier with chocolate

strawberries, cupcakes, Christmas

and Hanukkah cookies. There was also the traditional

English fruit cake and carrot cake.

As the dinner was ending, George gathered the guests and told them it was time to open the Christmas Eve and Hanukkah gifts. The Guests followed George Rabbit to the foyer of the Victorian House.

"It's our own little tradition to pass out gifts for our friends and neighbors on Christmas Eve. The gifts have your names on them and have been placed under the Christmas tree and Hanukkah Bush." Before we begin opening the presents, the Cat family would like to sing a Family Hanukkah song and afterwards, please join them in the lighting of the first candle of Hanukkah," said George.

After the Hanukkah Song was sung and the first candle on the Menorah was lit, the Cat Family went to the Hanukkah Bush to open their gifts. The twins opened their gifts first. Callie got a puppet while Casey got blocks.

Callie and Casey ran up to Henry and said at the same time,

"Thank you for the Hanukkah gifts."

Callie turned to the other guests and said,
"If you like I could put on a puppet show?
I love putting on shows for my family."
The guests all laughed.
Casey was in front of the Hanukkah Bush playing
with his blocks. Yogi went up to Casey and asked him
what he was building.

Casey said, "I am building a fort to keep the soldiers
away from the castle. I need to keep the
King and Queen safe."

Cal and Cate went to Pat and George
and thanked them for the Gourmet Catnip Tea Set.

Pat said, "I am glad you like it.
George and I visited a Gourmet Shop
on Beatrix Island. The tea set came from France."

Cate said, "Cal and I love France,
we went there on our honeymoon.
It's a beautiful place to visit."

Wiley Mink was in tears when he saw his bed quilt.
He told Pat that he needed another bed quilt since his
was falling apart and he couldn't afford to get a new one.
Pat hugged Wiley and told him it was ok and that's what
neighbors are for, helping one another.

Yogi Pomeranian got a rugby ball (football).
Yogi jumped up and down yelping,
"I always wanted a rugby ball and it's signed by
rugby legend Mike "Pom Pom" Pomeranian."

Lidia told Pat that Yogi loves playing rugby and
dreams about being a professional rugby player.

When Lidia Pomeranian opened her gift and saw
the pearl necklace she was overcome with
emotions. She went over to Pat and hugged
her and said to Pat, "I told myself that one day
I would treat myself to a pearl necklace."

Pat replied, "Well, today is the day I treat you to a pearl necklace."

After the gifts were opened and Christmas Carols were sung,
the Rabbit Family gathered their guests and
passed out the Sparkling Cider.

George said, "Let's lift up our glasses.
From our family to your family,
I want to thank all of you for coming to our
annual Christmas Eve dinner!"

In unison, George, Pat, and Henry wished their guests a

Happy Christmas (United Kingdom),

Nadolig Llawen (Wales),

Merry Christmas (United States),

Happy Hanukkah, and a Happy New Year. Pat closed by saying, "Before you all go, there are hand printed recipe note cards from our Christmas Eve dinner on the table by the door."

The End!

LIKE MY BOOK?
CHECK OUT MY OTHER BOOKS!

-Teresa Stern

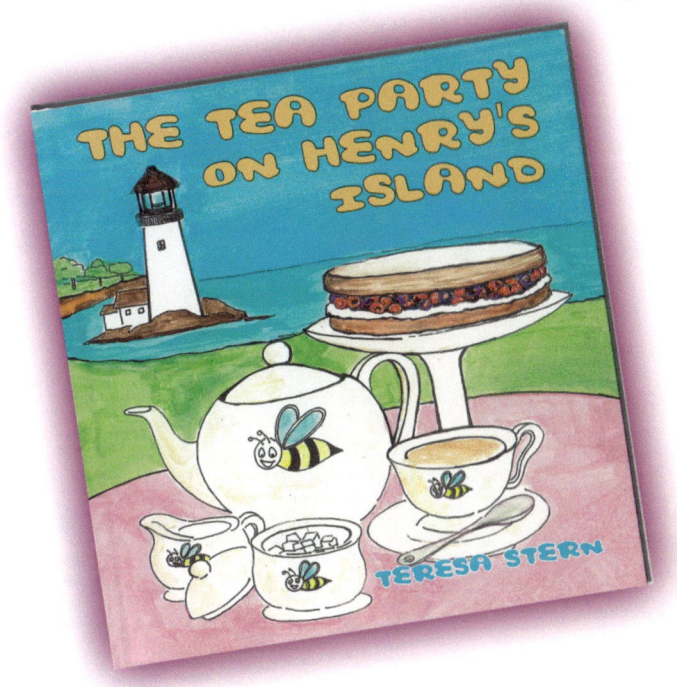

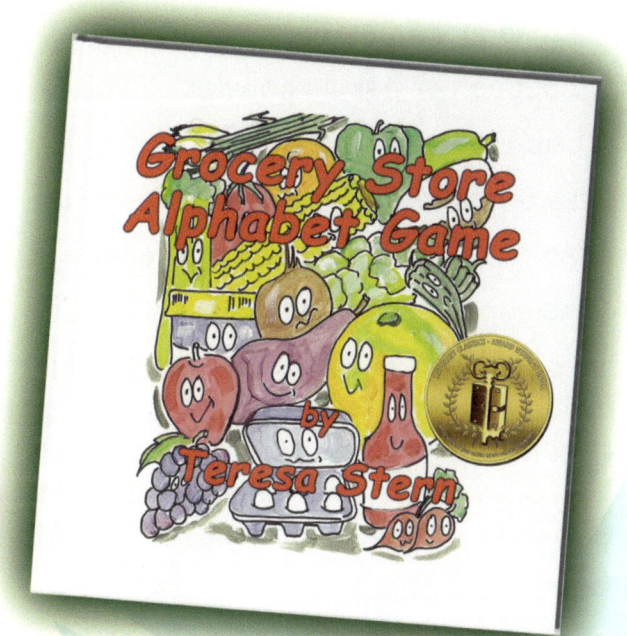

Available
at
Amazon and Barnes & Noble

www.teresaastern.com

Doris Rabbit's
Welsh Scones

Ingredients:

- 4 cup Gluten-Free oats, plus more for dusting (ground up in a food processor to make flour)

- 1/4 teaspoon of salt

- 1 teaspoon of baking powder

- 1/2 cup butter cut into cubes

  (May Substitute: Unsalted, Lactose-Free or Vegan butter).

- 4 tablespoons of powdered (or caster) sugar

- 4 tablespoons coconut sugar

- 1/3 cup of mixed dried fruit. Dried fruit includes: currents (in season June-August, raisins can be substituted for currents), figs, dried cherries or other dried fruits with dark chocolate morsels (Gluten-Free).

- 3/4 cup of buttermilk (milk substitutes include: Lactose-Free milk and/or Vegan milk)

- 1 teaspoon of vanilla extract

- A squeeze of lemon cut in half.

  (See Tip Below)
  1 beaten egg to glaze (optional)
  Jam and butter or jam and clotted
  cream to serve

Servings: 8 Prep: 15 minutes. Bake: 15 minutes.

Directions: Heat oven at 425F.

Tip the flour into a large bowl with the salt and baking powder, then mix and add dry mixed fruit together. Then add the butter and rub in with your fingers until the mix looks like fine crumbs and then stir in the sugar. Put the milk into a jug and heat in the microwave for about 30 seconds until warm, but not hot.
Then add the vanilla and lemon juice then set aside for a moment.
Put a baking tray and sheet in the oven.

Make a well in the dry mix,then add the liquid and combine it quickly witha cutlery knife. It will seem wet at first.
Scatter some flour onto the work surface and tip the dough out.
Dredge the dough and your hands with a little more flour, then fold the dough over 2-3 times until it is a little smoother then pat or roll into a round shape that is about 2 cm deep.

Take a 2 cm cutter (smooth-edged cutters tend to cut more cleanly, giving a better rise) and dip it into some flour. Plunge into the dough then repeat until you have four scones. By this point, you'll probably need to press what's left of the dough back into a round to cut out another four.Brush the tops with beaten egg then carefully place onto the hot baking tray and bake for 10 minutes until the scones have risen and are golden on the top.

Eat warm or cold on the day of baking with just butter and jam or generously topped with jam and clotted cream.If freezing the scones, freeze once the scones are cool. Defrost, then put scones in the oven on a low temperature (about 320F) for a few minutes to refresh.

Tip: Adding a squeeze from both halves of lemon to the milk sours it slightly, mimicking sharp-tasting milk (buttermilk), often used in scones. The slightly acidic mix gives a boost to the raising agents in the flour and baking powder.

Captain Isaac Lion's
Creamy Zucchini Soup

Ingredients:

- **10 tablespoons chopped onion**
- **16 tablespoons butter (May substitute: Unsalted, Lactose-Free or Vegan)**
- **16 tablespoons all-purpose flour (May substitute: rice flour or arrowroot for Gluten-Free option)**
- **5 cups whole milk (or milk substitute)**
- **5 cups water**
- **2 Knorr tubs Homestyle Vegetable Stock (May substitute: 7 cups of a different brand of vegetable stock)**
- **12 oz. Pacific Organic Condensed Cream of Mushroom Soup (Non-Dairy/Vegan) Imagine-Creamy Portobello Mushroom Soup or, Vivian's Live Again Creamy Mushroom Soup Mix** **(Online only at Amazon and, Vivian's Live Again)**
- **3 teaspoons of salt**
- **1 1/2 teaspoon pepper**
- **18 large zucchinis, shredded**
- **2 cups (16 ounces) Smoked Gouda cheese (May substitute: Goat cheese, Lactose-Free cheese or Vegan cheese)**

10 to 20 Servings. Prep: 10 minutes. Cook: 25 minutes.

Directions:

In a large soup pot, sauté onion in butter until tender.
Stir in flour until blended. Gradually stir in the milk, water,
vegetable stock, cream of mushroom condensed soup,
salt and pepper. Bring to a boil; cook and stir for 2 minutes or until thickened.

Add zucchini. Simmer uncovered
for 10 minutes or until zucchini is tender.
Stir in cheese until melted.

Garnish with fresh
herbs and zucchini circles.

Della Blue Bird's
Meat Potato Pie

Ingredients:

- 2 cups shredded peeled potatoes
  (about 1 pound)
  (May substitute: sweet potatoes)
- 1-1/2 cups (6 ounces) shredded Swiss
  cheese, divided (May substitute:
  Goat cheese or Lactose-Free cheese)
- 1 teaspoon salt, divided
- 2 eggs
- 1/2 cup milk (or milk substitute)
- 1 cup cooked, seasoned ground turkey
  (see seasonings for ground turkey below)
  (May substitute: ground beef or ground chicken)
- 1/2 cup chopped onion
- 1/2 teaspoon pepper
- 3 oz. vegetable oil or coconut oil in
  a frying pan
- Season the ground turkey with the
  following herbs before making the pie.

  > 1/4 teaspoon dill weed
  > 1/4 teaspoon rosemary
  > 1/4 teaspoon thyme
  > 1/4 teaspoon basil leaves
  > 1/4 teaspoon parsley

Servings: 6 to 8 Prep: 15 minutes. Bake: 45 minutes.

Directions:

Combine potatoes, 1/2 cup cheese and 1/2 teaspoon salt.
Press onto the bottom and up the sides of a greased 9-inch pie plate.

In a bowl, beat eggs and milk. Add seasoned turkey, onion,
pepper and remaining cheese and salt; pour over potato crust
(dish will be very full).

Bake at 350° for 45-50 minutes or until a knife inserted near
the center comes out clean. Let stand for 5 minutes before cutting.

Lebby Butterfly's
Veggie Sweet Potato Pie

Ingredients:

- 2 cups shredded, peeled sweet potatoes (about 1 pound)
- 1-1/2 cups (6 ounces) crumbled or creamy goat cheese, divided
- 1 teaspoon salt, divided
- 2 eggs
- 1/2 cup milk (or milk substitute)
- 1 cup sliced sautéed mushrooms
- 1/2 cup chopped onion
- 1/2 teaspoon pepper
- 3 oz. vegetable oil or coconut oil in a frying pan Sautée Mushrooms with the following

Seasonings:

    1/4 teaspoon dill weed

    1/4 teaspoon rosemary

    1/4 teaspoon thyme

    1/4 teaspoon basil leaves

    1/4 teaspoon parsley

Servings: 6 to 8 Prep: 15 minutes. Bake: 45 minutes.

Directions:

Combine potatoes, 1/2 cup cheese and 1/2 teaspoon salt.
Press onto the bottom and up the sides of a greased 9-inch pie plate.

In a bowl, beat eggs and milk. Add sautéed mushrooms, onion, pepper, dill weed, rosemary, thyme, basil leaves, parsley and the remaining cheese and salt; pour over potato crust (dish will be very full).

Bake at 350° for 45-50 minutes or until a knife inserted near the center comes out clean.
Let stand for 5 minutes before cutting.

* Optional: Garnish with extra
goat cheese over pie.

Teri Butterfly's
Cheese Potato Pie

Ingredients:

- **2 cups shredded, peeled potatoes (about 1 pound) (May substitute: sweet potato)**

- **1-1/2 cups (6 ounces) shredded Smoked Gouda cheese, divided (May substitute: Goat cheese, Lactose-Free cheese)**

- **1 teaspoon salt, divided**
- **2 eggs**
- **1/2 cup milk (or milk substitute)**
- **1/2 cup chopped onion**
- **1/2 teaspoon pepper**
- **1/4 teaspoon dill weed**
- **1/4 teaspoon rosemary**
- **1/4 teaspoon thyme**
- **1/4 teaspoon basil leaves**
- **1/4 teaspoon parsley**

Directions:

Combine potatoes, 1/2 cup cheese and 1/2 teaspoon salt.
Press onto the bottom and up the sides of a greased 9-inch pie plate.

In a bowl, beat eggs and milk. Add seasonings: onion, pepper, dill weed, rosemary, thyme, basil leaves, parsley and the remaining cheese and salt; pour over potato crust (dish will be very full).

Bake at 350° for 45-50 minutes or until a knife inserted
near the center comes out clean. Let stand for 5 minutes before cutting.

Rabbi Shawn Butterfly's
Salmon Mousses

Ingredients:

- Nonstick cooking spray
- 1/4 cup cold water
- 1 envelope Knox Original Gelatin Unflavored (2 teaspoons)
- 2 tablespoons chili and garlic sauce
- 2 tablespoons sweet chili sauce (mixed together).
- 1/4 teaspoon curry
- 1 cup plain low-fat yogurt (May substitute: Lactose-Free)
- 1 package (8 ounces) Philadelphia Cream Cheese at room temperature (May substitute: Lactose-Free)
- 1 teaspoon dried fine herbs or thyme
- 1/4 teaspoon black pepper
- 8 ounces Vita Classic Smoked Atlantic Nova Salmon or Lox
- 1/4 cup finely chopped celery
- 1/4 cup finely chopped pimiento-stuffed green olives

Servings. 24   **Prep Time:** 10 minutes. **Cooking Time:** 5 minutes.
Standing Time: 15 minutes. **Chilling Time:** 3 hours.

Directions:

Coat 3-cup decorative mold with cooking spray; set aside.
Put the cold water in small saucepan; sprinkle gelatin on top.
Let stand 1 minute to soften. Stir in chili sauce and curry.
Cook over moderate heat for 5 minutes or until gelatin is
completely dissolved. Transfer to a medium-size bowl;
let stand at room temperature for 15 minutes.

Add yogurt, Philadelphia Cream Cheese, fines herbs and pepper.
With an electric mixer on high, beat until creamy. Fold in salmon, celery and olives.
Spoon into a mold. Cover with plastic wrap and refrigerate for 3 hours or overnight
until it has set. Unmold onto a plate. Served with Matzo Crackers.

Note:
Small Koi Fish Plastic Mold makes 4 to 5 servings.
Available online.

www.ingramcontent.com/pod-product-compliance
Lightning Source LLC
Chambersburg PA
CBHW041556120626
46551CB00002B/228